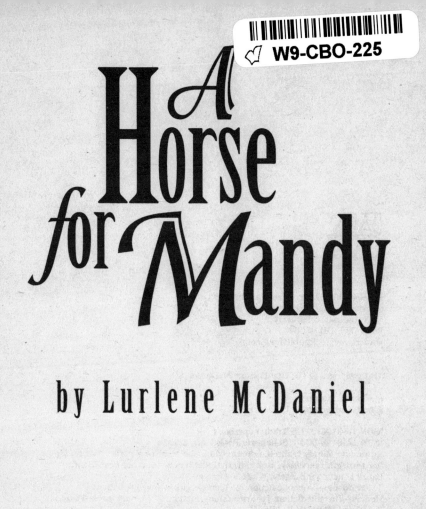

A Horse for Mandy

by Lurlene McDaniel

DARBY CREEK PUBLISHING

Published by Darby Creek Publishing,
a division of Oxford Resources, Inc.
7858 Industrial Parkway
Plain City, OH 43064
www.darbycreekpublishing.com

Text copyright © 1981 by Lurlene McDaniel

McDaniel, Lurlene.
A horse for Mandy / by Lurlene McDaniel.
    p. ; cm.
ISBN 1-58196-011-5 Trade paperback
ISBN 1-58196-024-7 Scholastic Book Fairs Edition
Summary: Mandy realizes a dream when she receives a horse, Solana, for
her thirteenth birthday. But, now that she has Solana, her best friend,
Laura is acting strangely. What is going on?
1. Friendship—Juvenile fiction. 2. Teenage girls—Juvenile fiction. 3.
Horses—Juvenile fiction. [1. Friendship—Fiction. 2. Teenage girls—Fiction.
3. Horses—Fiction.] I. Title.
PZ7.M4784172 Ho 2004
[Fic] dc22
OCLC: 54845604

Printed in the United States of America

Sixth printing
6 8 10 9 7

Solana heard the noise first. The little horse pricked up her short, sensitive ears and gave a nervous snort.

"What is it, girl?" Mandy asked. She strained to hear what Solana was hearing.

There! It sounded like a moan, Mandy thought. No . . . just the creek. No . . . it *was* a moan! Mandy began groping along on her hands and knees in the wet, thick undergrowth. The banks of the creek rose steeply. She could see the edge of the trail above whenever she looked up.

Mandy's hand touched something soft. And at the same time, she saw a bright patch of cloth. *It's Laura!* she thought.

My deepest appreciation to Doug and Glee Jones,
without whose help this book could not have been written.
Also thank you to Tina Tucker, Laura Cammeron,
Roger Smith, and of course, to Kathy Carter
and her "flying fingers."

One

"CAN you believe it?" Mandy shouted into the phone. "My very own horse!" She could just imagine Laura Callahan's face on the other end of the phone. Rich, proud Laura Callahan—who had grown up with a whole stableful of beautiful horses. But today, on her thirteenth birthday, Mandy Wilson's dream of owning her very own horse finally had come true.

"Isn't Dad terrific?" Mandy asked. Then she hurried on, not waiting for an answer. "Isn't that the neatest birthday present ever? I mean, I had no idea. He just surprised me."

Mandy stopped for a breath and Laura asked, "What breed? A Tennessee Walker, like Diablo?"

Mandy thought of Laura's big red-gold Tennessee Walker. How often she had longed to have him for her own. "No, not a Walker. Her name is Solana. Dad says she's a Paso Fino."

For a minute, Laura said nothing. Then, "Oh, one of *them*." Something in the sound of her voice made Mandy angry. But she swallowed hard and said nothing. She wasn't about to let Laura spoil her birthday!

"Anyway," Mandy continued, a little less eagerly, "we're heading out to your house and stables in a few minutes so I can see my horse. I—I thought you might like to meet us down by the stalls."

"Well, of course, I would!" Laura's voice changed and she once again seemed her old friendly self. "When will you be there?"

Just then Mandy's father stuck his head into her room. "Ready?" he asked.

Mandy nodded her head excitedly. "We're leaving in just a few minutes. Meet you at the stables in half an hour," she said into the phone.

"You bet!" said Laura and she hung up.

Mandy leaped off her bed and threw her arms around her father. "Oh, Dad, thanks! It's the best present in the whole world."

Bud Wilson ruffled his daughter's sandy blond hair and tapped her turned-up nose. "Anything for you, Princess," he said. Mandy reminded him so much of her mother. Blond hair, sparkling blue eyes, full of life and love . . . he shook off the memory. It was hard to believe that Mandy's mother, Ruth, had died more than eight years before.

"Dad?" Mandy asked.

"Huh?"

"You looked so far away. I said, 'Could we go now?'"

"Sorry, honey. Sure. Let's go see your birthday present."

During the ride, Mandy thought about the summer. June was her favorite month. Not just because it was her birthday month, either. Because school was out and she could spend every waking hour at the Callahan stables. She could ride, groom the horses, and help her father with his veterinarian duties whenever he needed her.

Mandy couldn't remember a time when she hadn't been around horses. But now, to have her very own horse was almost more than she could stand. Her dad had always promised her one. "When I feel you're old enough to have the responsibility" is what he'd always told her. So today she was doubly proud. Her dad trusted her to care for her very own horse.

A half hour later she got out of the car. She swung open the big gate leading to the Callahan home and nearby stables. Mandy felt like running ahead. Instead she scooted back into the car and rode the rest of the way up the Callahan driveway. But when they both got out and began to walk over toward one of the stable buildings, Mandy could wait no longer. She ran forward eagerly.

"Wait for me, young lady!" her dad called after her. "You don't even know what stall she's in."

"Oh, Dad!" Mandy cried. "You're so slow!"

"I'm so OLD!" he laughed. "It's the third stall over, honey. But slow down. Don't scare her to death."

Mandy looked inside at her horse. Solana de Omega. Mandy was sure that she had never seen anything quite as beautiful. Solana had all the fine lines of the Paso Fino breed: short inward-curved ears; large, wide-spaced eyes with a gentle expression; and a thick, arched neck—all of the finest features. She was a buckskin, too. Creamy yellow in color, with a black mane, tail, and stockings. "Oh, Daddy," Mandy whispered, "she's SO perfect!"

Solana's natural curiosity brought her over to the door of the stall. Mandy stroked her soft muzzle.

Dr. Wilson looked pleased. He said, "She's a great little horse, honey. Pasos are very affec-tion-ate, you know. Sometimes they act more like puppies than horses. She'll follow you around once she gets attached to you. They're very intelligent, too."

"Can I ride her right now?" Mandy asked eagerly. Then her face fell. "Oh, no. I don't have any tack." Mandy knew how expensive saddles and bridles were.

"That's the best part about Pasos," her

father said. "Solana can be ridden with a rope rein. Here, slip this on her." He removed a handmade rope rein from a nail next to Solana's stall.

Mandy opened the stall door, slipped the gear over Solana's head, and led the horse outside. Dr. Wilson gave her a leg up, and Mandy sat tall on Solana's bare back. "Go on, Mandy. Give her her head."

Mandy clucked softly and Solana began a smooth, natural, relaxed gait. As Mandy rode around the yard she marveled at how comfortable Solana's gait was. There was no teeth-jarring bouncing like other saddle horses, just a smooth, flowing ride.

Suddenly, Mandy saw the familiar form of her friend Laura hanging over the pasture fence. She tugged slightly on the left of the rope rein. Solana responded instantly and headed toward the fence. Mandy pulled her to a stop in front of Laura.

"Well, what do you think? Isn't Solana just beautiful?" Mandy asked eagerly.

"She's okay," Laura offered. "Kind of a runt, though, don't you think?"

Two

"WHAT do you mean?" Mandy asked. She felt her cheeks become flushed with anger.

"Oh, nothing," Laura shrugged. "She seems so much smaller than Diablo."

"Well, she is a lot smaller than Diablo," said Mandy. "Pasos only stand about thirteen to fifteen hands high."

Laura eyed Solana, mentally measuring the distance between the ground and the top of her shoulders. "I guess she's less than fourteen hands," she said. "Diablo measures in at sixteen."

"Do you want to ride with me?" Mandy asked, changing the subject.

"Sure. Let me saddle up."

Mandy watched Laura trudge off toward Diablo's stall. Mandy still felt a little hurt by Laura's attitude. After all the times they'd taken turns riding Diablo, Mandy thought that Laura would be thrilled that Mandy had her own horse. Why would Laura act this way? Mandy wondered. She again turned the problem over and over in her mind.

Mandy remembered all the summers she and Laura had groomed Diablo together, preparing him for the fall circuit shows. And she remembered how proud she had felt when they had brought home the coveted blue ribbons. She also remembered how tall Laura sat on Diablo in the shows . . . how smoothly he went through his classic gaits . . . how thrilled she felt whenever the judges called out Diablo's name as Best in Show.

Her thoughts were interrupted by Laura riding up on the big red-gold stallion. He snorted and pawed the ground restlessly. Solana responded with her own soft whinny.

Laura looked good sitting high in her Plantation saddle. Mandy felt a little dwarfed on Solana's bare back. But she clucked loudly and the little Paso Fino responded at once.

Together the two girls rode their horses around the Callahans' front yard. The Walker shifted into his distinctive running walk and the Paso into her smooth-flowing gait. Mandy felt her spirits soaring. She was certain that this was the happiest moment of her whole life. She was riding her own horse, chasing the wind through a sunlit June afternoon.

When they finally reined in their mounts, Mandy turned excitedly to Laura. "Isn't this wonderful?" Mandy asked.

But Laura seemed distant. "Of course," she said. Yet Mandy couldn't help but sense that something was wrong.

"Listen," said Laura, "meet me back at the house in a few minutes." She dug her heels into Diablo's side and galloped off. Mandy felt hurt and bewildered.

Later, back at Solana's stall, Mandy

groomed her horse expertly. But she couldn't keep her mind off her friend. She brushed Solana's buttercolored coat, untangled her black mane, and mulled over her own thoughts.

She had been Laura's friend since third grade. That was when her father first began practicing in Devonshire and became the veterinarian at the Callahan Stables. She remembered how unpopular Laura had been at school. "Snotty" was what most of the other girls had called Laura Callahan. She was a loner—keeping to herself, her nose in a book. At first Mandy had thought she was just shy. But later she realized that Laura chose not to be a part of the crowd that giggled and whispered together in the lunchroom.

Then, during that first summer, Mandy went with her father to the Callahan Stables. She got to know Laura better. Their mutual love of horses brought them together. They rode and groomed and fussed over all kinds of horses. Mandy realized that Laura had dreams of becoming a real horsewoman. Laura wanted to ride great show animals and collect trophies and ribbons.

When Laura was in the fourth grade, her parents gave her Diablo, a show-winning Tennessee Walker. What fun the two girls had had with him! Laura had never minded sharing her horse with Mandy. She even encouraged her friend to ride him.

That was why Laura's behavior this morning had been so baffling to Mandy. Didn't Laura know that now they could have more fun than ever? They could ride together without having to take turns. They could go off on picnics, each on her own horse.

She brushed and brushed Solana's coat until it gleamed.

"You're going to brush the fur right off her, if you're not careful." The deep masculine voice startled her. She jumped and dropped the grooming brush.

Mandy whirled around and looked into the bluest eyes she'd ever seen. "Sorry, I didn't mean to scare you," the blue-eyed, blond boy said. "My name is David Mannington. Who are you?"

Three

"I—I'M Mandy," she stuttered, feeling her face turn red. Suddenly she stooped to retrieve the brush. But David had the same idea. Their hands touched, and their heads bumped. Mandy dropped the brush again. "Oh, my goodness . . ."

David began to laugh, his blue eyes dancing. "We haven't gotten off to a very good start, have we?"

Mandy was still too flustered to say anything. She backed up into the safety of Solana. But the sound of David's laughter got to her. She started to giggle. "No, I guess not."

"Then let's start over again," he said. "I'm

David. And you're Mandy. This, I take it, is your horse?"

"Why, yes," Mandy said, still not daring to look him straight in the eye. "This is Solana. She's my birthday present."

"Well, happy birthday. Are you stabling her here?" he asked.

"Yes. My father is Doc Wilson. He looks after the Callahan ranch. Are you keeping a horse here?"

He reached over and patted Solana. "No, I'm working here this summer . . . you know, helping out. I'm new here. We just moved in on York Street. Thought I'd better get a job so I can buy school clothes . . . you know, stuff. Get to know some of the kids, too. You go to school in town?"

Mandy finally began to regain her composure. "Yes. I mean, I'll be at the middle school this fall."

"Great!" David said. "Then I already know somebody. I'm starting eighth grade there. Know anything about the track team?"

Before she could answer, Laura walked up.

"I've been waiting forever at the house. What's keeping . . ." Her voice trailed off when she saw David.

"Hi," he said. "I'm David Mannington."

"I'm Laura Callahan." Mandy could tell that he was having the same effect on Laura that he was having on her. "Are you the new hand Daddy hired?" Laura asked in an icy voice.

"Sure am."

"Then don't you have anything better to do?"

He stood up straight and looked down on both girls. "You're right. See you later, Mandy." He nodded, then walked off.

"Really, Laura, that wasn't a very nice way to treat him. He's new in town and just wanted to get to know about school and all," Mandy said after David was gone.

"Oh, don't be so touchy. It's better I tell him to get to work than Daddy. We can talk to him later. You finished cooling Solana?"

Mandy shrugged. "Sure."

"Then, come on in the house and have some lunch with me."

Mandy trudged behind her to the house, but she was still a little angry. Why did Laura always treat people like they were inferior to her? The Callahans had plenty of money, and she'd heard it said that they "owned the town." But that was no reason to treat people like lower life forms.

When they walked into the kitchen, all of Mandy's anger evaporated. In the center of the table sat a beautiful birthday cake, blazing with candles.

"Happy birthday!" shouted Laura, clapping her hands with glee. "Are you surprised? Did you think I'd forgotten?"

Tears sprang to Mandy's eyes. "Oh, Laura, it's gorgeous. Thanks so much." She hugged her friend and hated herself for all her mean thoughts about Laura. Mandy made a wish and blew out the candles.

"Look!" Laura said. "Here's your present." She handed Mandy a carefully wrapped gift, topped with a bright red bow. "I picked this out for both of us really. Come on. Open it."

Mandy tore open the box excitedly. Inside lay two bright-colored scarves. "Oh, Laura! How beautiful!"

"Do you like them? Really? The red one's yours. The blue one's mine. They're a symbol of our friendship. Will you always wear yours?"

"You bet!" Mandy tied the scarf around her neck, Western fashion. "Hey, I have an idea," Mandy said eagerly. "Why don't we fix a picnic lunch and take it out on the trail? We could ride our horses and eat down by the creek."

"Sure. That sounds like fun," Laura agreed.

So the rest of Mandy's thirteenth birthday was spent with her best friend, her own horse, and the ants that showed up for the picnic. Looking back, Mandy thought it was one of the best times she had ever had. And it was just as well that she didn't know what was coming next.

Four

THE next few weeks passed quickly. July came. Mandy's days were filled from dawn to dark with Solana and life at the Callahan Stables. She saw David almost every time she was there. Her reaction to him surprised her.

Her heart would pound and she would often blush when he so much as smiled at her. She found herself looking forward to seeing his lanky build, his blond hair, and his casual half-smile. Most of all she liked talking with him.

She and Laura rode the trails together, but Mandy could sense a kind of wall building up between them. What was happening to them and their friendship? Mandy wondered.

If it hadn't been for Solana and David, Mandy might have stopped going to Callahans' altogether. Her father had been right. The Paso was affectionate and smart. Now, whenever Mandy came, Solana greeted her with snorts and whinnies. The horse was so attached to Mandy that she followed her owner everywhere. In fact, if Mandy didn't lock the gate firmly, Solana would follow her dad's car home. Even when the horse was grazing, just one sharp whistle from Mandy would bring her rushing over.

Mandy couldn't help but notice that Diablo wasn't like that with Laura. No, the big stallion was fine in the show ring and great on the trail, but he wasn't affectionate and gentle like Solana. Maybe this was what was coming between them, Mandy thought.

She was watering Solana one afternoon when her father paused next to her. "Penny for your thoughts?" he asked.

"Oh, Dad. I don't know. It's just that . . . that Laura and I don't seem to be really good friends anymore," Mandy told him.

Dr. Wilson stopped and leaned against the stable wall. "Really? You seem to be everywhere together, always riding, talking. What do you mean?"

"I don't know. It's just that Laura seems . . . kinda mean about Solana. I mean, I thought she'd be thrilled because I had my own horse. But she's not. And then there's David . . ." Her voice trailed off, and Mandy felt herself begin to blush.

If her dad noticed, he didn't say anything. "Well, honey," he began, "you and Laura are growing up. You're both turning into young women. It's only natural that your interests would change."

"But I'm still the same!" Mandy cried defensively. "She's the one who's jealous!"

"Mandy," her father said, "how would you feel if Solana suddenly took off with someone else? Started spending all her time with a new friend? How do you think you'd feel?"

Mandy thought hard about it for a moment. "I guess I'd be hurt," she said.

"That's right. And Laura will get over it. It's just too bad she never made more friends than you. Did you ever encourage her to do that? Or did you kind of keep her all to yourself and let her feel that she was the most important person in the world to you?"

Mandy felt a lump rise in her throat. Why, that's exactly what she'd done! In all the years, she'd never thought to invite any other girl into her and Laura's summers. It had always been just the two of them. No wonder Laura was feeling left out and lonely.

"Thanks, Dad," she said. "I guess I never looked at it that way before."

"I know. It's tough to be thirteen, honey." Then he leaned over to her, his eyes twinkling. "That's why I'm glad I'm creaking along in my forties."

"Oh, Dad . . ." Mandy laughed and watched him walk away. "Come on, Solana," Mandy said to her horse, and Solana obediently tagged along behind her. "Let's find Laura and go for a ride."

She checked Diablo's stall. The stallion was there alone, contentedly chewing on some hay. Mandy tied her birthday scarf around her neck, crossed the wide green lawn, and headed for the house. Laura wasn't in her room, nor was she on the back patio. Then Mandy remembered the lake far off behind the house. Surely, she'd be down there.

"Go on, Solana," Mandy said, stamping her foot. "Go eat some grass and stop following me."

Solana pricked her ears forward and then lowered her head and began to graze. Mandy walked toward the lake.

She was just about to call Laura's name when she heard the sound of laughter. She strained to see around a tree and then stopped dead in her tracks. There, facing the lake, with her back to Mandy, sat Laura. She was holding hands with David.

Mandy had never felt so many emotions in such a short time as she felt right then— surprise, hurt, betrayal, anger, sadness, then the urge to get out of there. But her foot cracked a branch. David and Laura turned at once with the sound.

"S-s-sorry!" Mandy stammered. "I was looking for you, Laura."

David stood up and pulled Laura up with him. "That's okay," he said casually. "I've got to get back to work. Thanks for the company, Laura." Then he strode off toward the stables.

Mandy and Laura stood facing each other. "I thought you were alone," said Mandy weakly.

"Well, I wasn't," Laura snapped, walking briskly past her.

"Wait up!" Mandy called and fell into step beside her. "I'm sorry, Laura. I thought that you didn't even know David was alive. I mean you've always treated him like he didn't even exist."

"Look, Mandy, just because you're jealous—"

"Jealous!" Mandy exploded. "Me? Why, *you're* the one who's moped around here all summer long, treating me like I've committed some crime because I got my own horse. And *you're* the one who made me feel dumb just talking to David . . ."

"You just stop it, Mandy Wilson!" Laura yelled back. "I could care less about your stupid little horse. I own a real show horse, not some squatty little saddle pony. And as for David . . . well, it's obvious that he prefers me to you."

Mandy stopped dead, the tears springing to her eyes. "You're so mean, Laura. I hope that I never have to talk to you again!"

"Well, that goes double for me!" Laura shout-ed back. Then she ran toward her house. Mandy stood shaking for a long time after she had left.

Suddenly, the day was a disaster. As she headed back toward the stables, Mandy couldn't help but feel she'd lost something special.

She found herself back at the stable and then felt a warm muzzle in the middle of her back. With a start she turned around and realized that Solana had been following behind her all along. She buried her face in her horse's mane and began to cry.

"You're so lucky, Solana," Mandy said

between sobs. "You don't know what it's like to be a person." Solana snorted.

Mandy remembered Laura's angry words again. She thought of her mixed-up feelings at seeing Laura and David together. Why should that bother her so much? She and David had talked lots of times, and Laura didn't seem to notice. This was silly. Could she have a crush on him?

No, she was just mad at Laura, she thought. Absentmindedly, Mandy led Solana into her stall. She turned to fasten the rope door. But her mind was far away. Her fingers fumbled at a job she should have been able to do in her sleep. She turned and walked away, not realizing the knot was only half tied.

Five

"**H**EY, Solana! Come on, you lazy nag. . . let's go for a ride." Mandy began calling to her horse as she walked toward the stall door. There was no familiar answering snort. In fact, the closer she got to the stall, the stranger things seemed.

Solana's stall was empty. Mandy couldn't imagine where she was. She remembered roping up the door the day before. But the ropes were untied and Solana was not in her stall.

"Who could . . . ?" Mandy wondered out loud, looking at the dangling ropes. Then she ran out into the yard and began to whistle. From behind the stable Mandy heard a feeble whinny.

"Solana! What are you doing there?" she asked, running around the stable. Mandy stopped suddenly. There was Solana all right, but her head was drooping and she seemed shaky on her legs. "What's the matter?" Mandy anxiously ran to her horse. Solana could hardly walk. She was limping terribly. It took them almost ten minutes to cover the short distance back to her stall.

Inside, Mandy picked up Solana's left foreleg and searched the hoof for damage. She could see nothing. No cuts, no thorns . . . but it was swollen. "Stay, Solana!" Mandy cried in alarm. "I'll go find Dad."

Dr. Wilson rushed back with his daughter in a matter of minutes. "Oh, Dad, what's wrong? Can't you help her?" Mandy began to cry softly.

He examined the horse carefully. "Honey, I'm afraid its Laminitis—Founder." He shook his head grimly at his own diagnosis.

Mandy had been a vet's daughter too long not to understand what that meant. "Founder! Oh, no . . ." Mandy choked back her sobs. "But that could mean . . ." Her voice trailed off. She couldn't say the words.

"That could mean permanent crippling. Maybe even putting her down," he finished grimly.

"No! Can't you do something?" But she already knew the answer to that, too.

"Honey," Dr. Wilson explained, holding her by the shoulders. "You know that this is something that has to run its course. There's a lot of congestion in her foot right now. The blood flow is very heavy. It's jammed up and she's hurting. But at least it's not infected. We can do something to prevent that. We'll start antibiotics. I'll give her a shot of adrenaline, too, in this leg. Maybe that will slow the flow of the blood and help the pain."

"Isn't there anything I can do to help?" Mandy begged.

"Yes, there is. You can start applying ice to both these front feet. And plan to spend day and night here, too."

The rest of the day seemed like a nightmare.

Her father did all he could. Then Mandy began the long nursing process. She brought an ice chest to Solana's stall and packed ice around her feet every hour. Mandy petted her and encouraged her to eat. Still her horse stood painfully and stared at the floor of her stall.

"Need some help?" She looked up into David's worried face.

"No, but thank you," Mandy said. He stood for a while making small talk. His being there lifted her spirits a lot.

It was almost suppertime before Mandy realized that Laura had not come by once to check on her. The thought upset her. Bitterly she changed Solana's ice. Of course, Laura knew. Everybody on the whole ranch seemed to know. Even Mr. Callahan had stopped by to check on her and comfort her. But not Laura.

When her father arrived with a take-out hamburger dinner, Mandy was still fuming. She didn't say anything to him, but ate in silence.

"Founder is a funny thing," he began, thinking her silence was worry. "A horse can recover from it as quickly as that." He snapped his fingers. "It goes as fast as it comes. Yesterday, Solana was fine—today Founder—tomorrow, perfectly well. What troubles me is how she got it. I know how careful you are with her, honey."

"What are some of the causes?" Mandy asked.

"Excessive work. Can't be that though. We all know how you spoil that filly. Idleness and lack of exercise, too. Couldn't be that either. Improper shoeing. . . but Solana doesn't even have shoes. Digestive disturbance is a big cause. You know, too much protein-rich feed."

Mandy's heart fell.

"What's wrong, honey?"

"Dad, when I came this morning, Solana wasn't in her stall."

"Where was she?"

"Wandering out back."

"Did you check the feed bin?"

"No . . . I never thought . . ."

"Mandy!" Her father was angry. "She got out of her stall and got into the sweet feed. I'll bet you anything. Mandy, how could you have been so careless? What could you have been thinking of when you put her in her stall last night?"

Mandy hung her head and began to cry. It was all her fault! If she'd had her mind on Solana yesterday instead of Laura and David, this never would have happened. *Oh, poor Solana*, Mandy thought. *Suffering so much and all because of me.*

"I'm sorry, Mandy," her father said gravely. "But this is very serious. I gave you a horse because I thought you'd be old enough to handle the responsibility."

The more she cried, the worse she felt. Her father reached over and put his arms around her. "Mandy, I'm sorry. I know you love Solana. I shouldn't have come down so hard on you. Look, you've been a real nurse today. You keep wrapping her feet tonight and I'll bet she'll be fine by morning."

Mandy wiped her eyes. "Sure," she said. "Did you bring my sleeping bag?"

"Right here," he told her, gesturing to the

corner of the stall. "Listen, the Callahans are letting me sleep up at the house tonight. If you have any problems, you come get me."

"Thanks, Dad." Mandy smiled weakly. Then she kissed him and watched him head up toward the house. She sighed and turned back to Solana. Mandy rolled out her sleeping bag. But she was certain that she wouldn't sleep tonight.

Six

MANDY watched the stars come out in twos, fours, and then in clusters. They twinkled brightly and coldly down at her. Over and over, she iced down Solana's swollen forefeet. Her heart soared when the horse nibbled on a little bit of feed.

"Good girl!" she said encouragingly. The lights were out at the Callahan house, and Mandy lost all track of time. Then she heard a scraping noise from farther down the stables. She bravely stepped out of Solana's stall to investigate and came face to face with Laura.

"What . . .?" she began.

"Oh, you startled me!" Laura exclaimed.

"Well, I'm spending the night here to keep an eye on Solana," Mandy explained. "I thought you were coming down here to check on us."

"I've been very busy . . . ," Laura started lamely.

"Busy?" Mandy asked coldly. "I would have come to see you if it had been Diablo."

"Oh, for goodness sake," began Laura haughtily, "it's not the end of the world. Why, I heard your dad tell my dad tonight that he thought your horse would be fine by morning."

"I'll bet that really bugs you." Mandy was angry.

"What's that supposed to mean?"

"You'd just love it if Solana would be crippled! Even put to sleep!"

"That's not true!" Laura shouted back.

"It is so! You've hated me having my own horse."

"And I always thought you were my best friend," Laura said, her eyes brimming with tears.

"Well, I'm NOT!" snapped Mandy. She was sorry immediately. But Laura turned and ran away before she could say anything else.

"Oh, Mandy . . . ," she yelled at herself, "how mean and rotten you are!" She knew she was mad at herself for neglecting Solana and letting the horse get sick in the first place. And she also knew that she was really just hurt and angry at Laura for not being her friend when she needed her. How different this day and night would have been if Laura had been here nursing Solana with her!

She went back inside the stall with a sigh and repacked the ice around Solana's feet. Mandy slept fitfully. The morning stars were beginning to fade when she awoke with a start.

She was cold. The morning was gray and damp. Immediately she checked Solana's feet. The swelling was gone. The horse looked perkier, too. "Dad was right. You're going to be fine, girl."

Mandy's legs felt stiff, so she decided to take a little walk. In no time she found herself down by the lake. The morning light made the water look soft and velvety.

"How's your horse?" It was David's voice. Mandy turned with a start. "I always seem to be scaring you," he said.

"Solana's better." She smiled. "It was a long night though."

Silence. Then, "You get any sleep?"

"Not really."

"You okay?"

"Oh, sure . . . ," she began, but tears started to slide down her cheeks.

"Hey," David said, putting his arm around her. "Everything's all right. Solana will be fine."

He felt so warm and comforting to her, and he smelled like fresh soap. "It's more than that." Her voice was muffled into his chest. "I had a big fight with Laura. I said some mean things."

"Oh." He continued to hold her and Mandy felt better. She was grateful he had come. The morning sun broke over the edge of the trees.

David started to speak and his voice soothed her. "You know, Laura really is an interesting girl. She told me all about how you two worked to get Diablo ready for all those horse shows.

She showed me all the ribbons and trophies she's won, too." He paused. "You know, I've run track for three years now. It's tough to win time after time. Laura's done that. She's gone into the ring against lots of competition. And more times than not, she's come out a winner."

Mandy pulled away from him. She swallowed hard and said, "So you think she's pretty terrific?"

"In some ways, yes. But don't you see? She's had to *not* care about a lot of other things to stay on top, to be a winner. I'll bet you're her only real friend."

"You mean *was* her only real friend."

"Naw. You can patch things up, if you try."

Mandy looked up into David's eyes. Her heart began to pound and she felt weak around the knees. He brushed her bangs back and cupped her chin softly in his hand, leaning toward her face.

"Mandy! Mandy!" Her father's voice cut through the morning air.

The spell was broken. She turned away, her

heart pounding in her ears. "Here, Dad! I 'm here!"

She ran toward him. "Here I am, Dad! Is it Solana? Is she okay?"

Dr. Wilson caught her by her arms. "Honey, have you seen Laura? Diablo's not in his stall, and Laura's bed wasn't slept in last night!"

Seven

"SEEN her? No! I mean, yes . . . ," Mandy stammered. "Late last night."

"What time? Where?" Mandy's father asked.

"Down by the stables. She came to check on Solana and me . . ." Mandy couldn't go on. She couldn't tell him about their fight. Where could Laura have gone? What had Mandy done?

"This is strange. She knows better than to go riding at night alone. It's very dangerous. Come on up to the house and talk to her parents. They're worried sick."

Mandy faced the Callahans and told again of Laura's late visit to the stables. "I don't like this," Mr. Callahan said, shaking his head.

"Martha, you call the Sheriff's Department. Bud, you come with me. We'll go round up some help and get a search party going."

"What if she's hurt?" asked Laura's mother.

"Don't think that way. We'll find her," Mr. Callahan assured his wife.

Mandy followed the two men out of the house toward the car. "Maybe I can help, too."

"Honey," her father said, "Solana's fine. But don't push her. Give her light exercise today. And stay put!" Then they were gone.

Mandy paced up and down the stable yard. Solana ate some hay and snorted eagerly to be let out. But Mandy's mind was in a whirl.

What had Laura been doing out so late last night? Had she really come down to the stables to check on Solana? Was she planning a night ride all along? Or had Mandy pushed her into it with her cutting words?

David was right. Laura *was* different. Ever since Mandy could remember, Laura had wanted to ride in the show ring. And Mandy had always been there helping her to go after her dream. But this summer, things had really been different. Mandy had spent all her time with her own horse, having fun instead of working and training with her friend.

And then there was David. It was obvious that they both had dreams about David. And it was obvious that David had chosen Laura. *Well, no time to think about that,* thought Mandy. *He understands Laura. And I come barging into their privacy just the other day. No wonder Laura was so upset.*

"Well," said Mandy to Solana, "I can't stand around here all day wishing the past away. Nobody knows the trails better than me and Laura." She thought about all the horseback exploring she and Laura had done over the years. No rescue party could find half of the places she and Laura knew about.

"Solana, we're going on a little trip." She slipped on Solana's rope rein and swung up onto the buckskin's smooth back. Then she headed out of the gate into the adjoining grassy field. She would have to make peace with her father later.

The sun beat down relentlessly. But the little Paso Fino gaited along without tiring. It was hard to believe that only yesterday she had been down with Founder. Mandy said a silent prayer that the ride wouldn't hurt Solana.

It seemed like hours passed. Up one trail. Down another. Mandy could hear the sounds of the search party. "Laura! Laura!" the men called. But the only answers were their own echoes fading in the summer air.

Mandy's stomach reminded her that she'd missed breakfast—and very likely lunch, too. But she couldn't go back. Suddenly, she heard the sound of talking and horses snorting. She rounded a bend in the trail and came on some of the search party having lunch. She looked directly into her father's surprised face.

"What in the blazes?" he asked.

"I'm sorry, Daddy," Mandy said, sliding off Solana's back. "But I just couldn't wait back at the house, doing nothing. Besides," she hurried on, "I know all of Laura's favorite places in these woods. I really think I can help."

He stared at her for a minute, then nodded. "You win. Come have some lunch and then we'll all take off again. How's Solana doing?"

"Fine, I think."

Dr. Wilson checked Solana over and nodded in satisfaction. Mandy sat down on the ground gratefully and quickly ate two sandwiches. She had started on an apple when her father finally spoke to her again.

"Got any ideas about where to look?"

"We used to like to go down by the creek a lot."

"We've looked there already—covered every inch above and below. Right now there are four separate parties out, mostly friends and neighbors. If we don't have any luck by morning, the sheriff will send in a group with dogs."

"Morning?" asked Mandy weakly. "Do you really think something's happened to her?"

"I don't know. But the longer it takes, the worse it looks."

Suddenly, a lone rider came trotting into their view. It was someone from another search party. He reined up short in front of Dr. Wilson. "We found her horse. He was grazing in a field about a mile from here. He has a slight limp. He must have thrown her. No telling how long he'd been wandering out there."

Mandy's stomach lurched.

"Saddle up!" Dr. Wilson ordered his group. "She's hurt all right."

Eight

RAIN! Its smell was in the afternoon air. Gray clouds scuttled across the sky and thunderheads boiled in from the north.

"This is lousy!" Dr. Wilson muttered. But Mandy knew it already. Rain would halt the search, end it before nightfall. Well, the others could turn back, but she wasn't going to! The constant thought of her friend lying hurt someplace made Mandy feel physically ill. She urged Solana on, and the Paso responded with unfaltering speed.

"Wait up!" her father called. "If we have to go back, don't get any ideas about going on without us," he told his daughter.

"I won't," Mandy said. She was aware that she had disobeyed him once already today. Yet, she purposely let more and more distance separate her from the rest of the party. Finally, around one bend she veered off west and headed toward the creek.

Somehow she had a feeling about the creek. In summers past, they'd had lots of picnics along its banks. Mandy really felt that Laura might have headed there the night before. The water would have erased Diablo's tracks. If she'd been thrown, she'd be lying down there, somewhere in the undergrowth and rocks.

Thunder rumbled and Solana strained to turn back for her stable.

"No, you don't, girl," Mandy said. "We're in this together—all the way."

The rain started with a dull drizzle, and in no time turned into a wicked downpour. The banks along the creek became very slippery. Mandy got off Solana and led her along the trail for safety's sake. They stopped for a while under a canopy of green leaves. Solana nibbled, and

Mandy waited for the rain to slack off.

By the time the rain stopped, it was dusk and darkness was coming fast. Still, Mandy led Solana around the creek bed. The rain had caused it to swell, and the water rushed loudly over stones and tree roots.

Solana heard the noise first. The little horse pricked up her short sensitive ears and gave a nervous snort.

"What is it, girl?" Mandy asked. She strained to hear what Solana was hearing.

There! It sounded like a moan, Mandy thought. No . . . just the creek. No . . . it *was* a moan! Mandy began groping along on her hands and knees in the wet, thick under-growth. The banks of the creek rose steeply. She could see the edge of the trail above when-ever she looked up.

Mandy's hand touched something soft. And at the same time, she saw a bright patch of cloth. *It's Laura!* she thought. Mandy pulled quickly at the undergrowth, throwing away chunks of bushes and tall, wet grass.

It was Laura all right. She was lying face-down and was covered with dirt and debris. Gently Mandy turned her over. Laura moaned again, but appeared to be unconscious. Her face was pale. She felt cold.

"Please, Laura, please, wake up! It's me. It's Mandy." She started to move Laura and then noticed the way her leg was bent backward. "It's broken. I just know it. Oh, no. What am I going to do?"

Mandy was worried. Should she leave Laura and go look for the search party? Mandy wondered. No, it was dark now. The searchers would have all gone back to the Callahans' to wait for morning. Maybe they would bring lights and keep on looking. Now *two* girls were missing.

Mandy imagined her father's face. She thought about how worried he must be. She began to cry. She was scared. Solana whinnied from far behind her. Solana! Of course! She'd send the horse back without her. That way they'd know she'd found Laura.

But how? Mandy hunted for some paper. There was nothing to write on. How could she let them know? They'd keep on looking if they could narrow down the places to look. How can I tell them? she wondered.

Mandy's eyes fell on the bright blue scarf around Laura's neck. Of course! The scarves. Everyone knew about the birthday present. Mandy pulled off her own scarf and then gently removed Laura's. She carefully tied up some small creek rocks in the red one and then went over to Solana.

"Here," she told her horse, tying both scarves to the horse's reins. "Now, go on back and get your supper." She led Solana back up the steep bank and turned her toward the Callahans' stable. "Please don't fool around, girl. I need you to go back to the stable." Mandy slapped Solana hard on the rump and sent her off at a fast pace. "Home!" she yelled.

Mandy watched her horse disappear out of sight. She hoped Solana's hunger and natural instinct would take her back to her warm, dry stable. She sighed and felt more alone than she ever had in her whole life. Then she thought of her friend lying hurt and unconscious below.

She scurried back down to her side.

Mandy knew enough about medicine to know that Laura was in bad shape. The way she had fallen, the twist of her leg, the color of her face left no doubt that she needed medical attention soon.

"Hurry, Solana," Mandy muttered under her breath. Then she hunted around for some way to make Laura more comfortable. She realized that the search party had probably passed Laura more than once that day. Because of the dense foliage, they had not seen her. With Laura drifting in and out of consciousness, she had probably never heard them calling her name either.

Mandy found some moss, shook it out and tried to cover Laura with it. She knew that it was important that Laura stay as warm as possible. Mandy's own clothes were damp and she began to feel chilly in the rain-cooled night air. But she sat huddled near Laura's head and settled down to wait out the long night ahead.

"Hurry, Solana," she whispered again.

Nine

TIME is hard to measure when you're alone in the dark. Mandy couldn't even guess how long she'd been sitting there when she heard Laura groan. Instantly, Mandy leaned over her.

"Here I am, Laura. It's Mandy. I'm right here and help is on the way."

"M—my leg . . . ," Laura whispered.

"I know. Don't try to move. We just have to hang on a little longer."

"What happened? How did you . . . ?" Her voice trailed off.

"I guess you were thrown. We've been looking for you all day. Me, Dad, your family—half the countryside, in fact. But it won't be long now." Mandy tried to sound reassuring.

"Yes. Now I remember . . ." Laura grimaced with pain. "Diablo tripped. A hole of some kind. I fell . . . Diablo!" Her voice rose in alarm.

"He's all right," Mandy said. "We found him this afternoon. He was limping, but Dad thought he'd be fine."

"That's good." Laura sighed. "How did you find me?"

"Just an idea I had. I remembered all the rides we used to take by the creek. I was just lucky."

Laura grew very quiet and Mandy became alarmed. She felt that she had to keep her talking. "Laura?"

There was a long silence before Mandy heard Laura say, "Yes?"

"Why did you go out riding alone at night? Was it because of the mean things I said to you?"

More silence. Then Laura answered softly, "Because everything you said was true. I hated it when you got your own horse. You spent all your time with your horse."

"I know. Oh, Laura, I'm so sorry. I was a rotten best friend. I didn't help you train once all summer for Diablo's fall show circuit. And David reminded me . . ."

The mention of David's name put up another wall between them. "David," Laura said painfully. "I wanted him to like me so much."

"Oh, but he does," Mandy urged eagerly. "Why, I saw you holding hands down by the lake. He even told me he likes you."

"I was holding his hand," Laura corrected. "But we were talking about you."

Mandy decided to change the subject. "Let me tell you how I sent for help." Quickly, she told how she'd tied their scarves on Solana's reins and sent the horse back. "I just hope she has the good sense to go home," she finished, half to herself.

Laura grew very quiet. "Laura," Mandy said, shaking her gently. "Don't slip away on me. Please, keep talking to me." But Laura did not respond.

Mandy scrambled to the edge of the creek

and dipped her hands into the cold water. She crawled back to Laura and patted her friend's face with the water.

Laura moaned. "I'm so cold . . ."

"I know. But it won't be long now." Mandy reassured her friend. She clutched her knees to her chest and prayed silently, "Oh, dear God, don't let it be long now. Please."

The night dragged on. Mandy tried to make Laura talk some more, but she only mumbled. Mandy found more moss and spread it over Laura, being very careful not to disturb the twisted leg. She went once more to the creek and took a long drink of water for herself. It helped refresh her, but did little to stop her growing hunger pangs.

Mandy began to think that when morning came she might have to set out on foot for help. She shuddered at the thought of leaving Laura out here alone. But she might have no choice. What if Solana had not made it back to the stable? What if she were off in some grassy field, wandering aimlessly?

"Well, I must stop thinking like that," she

told herself sharply. "Just take it one minute at a time. And try to get a little sleep." Just a little—why she hadn't been to sleep in her own bed for two nights now!

Two nights! The last forty-eight hours felt like ten years. How long ago it seemed since the start of the summer. How long ago since her birthday . . . Mandy drifted into a restless sleep.

In her dream, it was a brilliant white-hot day. She was standing and watching Solana graze in a large grassy field. She whistled and called to her over and over, but Solana acted as if she didn't hear. Yet, when Mandy tried to climb over the fence into the field, she discovered that it was so high she couldn't crawl over it. Helplessly, she called to her horse.

Then she saw Laura riding out into the field on Diablo. Mandy began to call to her frantically, but Laura couldn't hear her either. Slowly, Laura got off Diablo. She walked slowly over to Solana.

Laura petted her, then signaled to the little Paso. Solana followed her like a puppy. "No, no!" Mandy yelled in the dream. "She's my horse! Laura, don't! Solana is mine!" But they never heard her.

Just then, David walked into the field. He was smiling at Laura. He took her hand and together they began to walk away. Solana followed obediently behind them both. Mandy called and called to them.

The day was hot and still, the grass tall and swaying. No matter how hard she tried, she couldn't get over the fence. From out of nowhere, rows and rows of shiny trophies appeared, each engraved with Laura Callahan and Solana de Omega.

From very far away, Mandy heard someone calling her name. "Mandy! Mandy!" Over and over . . . David . . . her father . . . Laura . . . over and over . . .

Mandy struggled through layers and layers of sleep. Again, she heard her name. With a start, she sat up and realized that someone really *was* calling her name.

"Mandy!"

"Daddy!" she cried, struggling to her feet. "Daddy! Here I am! I'm down here, Daddy!"

From above the rim of the embankment, she saw a glowing yellow light. "Mandy! We're here, honey!"

Suddenly, the air was filled with voices, and her father was sliding down the steep incline. And suddenly he was there with her, hugging her to him. And she knew that she was safe— safe in her father's arms.

Ten

LOOKING back, Mandy was never really sure of what happened during the rest of that night and the next two days. She remembered anxious faces, many helping hands, the horse-drawn stretcher made for Laura. She didn't remember any of the ride back to the Callahans', only someone giving her hot tea in the Callahans' kitchen, then shedding her clothes and sliding between soft, flowered sheets.

Even the next morning, she could only vaguely recall the smell of bacon and coffee, a phone ringing, hushed voices and hours and hours of deep dreamless sleep. In fact, it was late the next afternoon before Mandy really woke up.

She awoke with a start and looked around the Callahans' guest bedroom. She got up and wandered down the hall and into the bright, sunny kitchen. Her father and the Callahans were sitting around the table with mugs of hot coffee.

"Mandy!" Her father grinned. "Welcome back. You've slept almost 'round the clock. Come on, honey. Have some food."

She sat numbly while Mrs. Callahan prepared her meal. Mandy listened to all the details of the past twenty-four hours.

"First of all, Laura's going to be fine," Mandy's dad assured her. "Her leg was badly broken. It's a good thing you didn't try to move her. She's in the hospital now. But she should be coming home tomorrow. Her leg will be in a cast for at least eight to ten weeks, but she will be fine."

"Oh, Dad, I'm so glad!" Mandy smiled.

"And you, young lady," he continued, "are something of a heroine. No, I mean it. That was quick thinking, Mandy, tying those scarves on Solana with the river rocks in them. That little filly made a beeline for home. Once we got your message, we gathered up some gear and lights and came right to you. I'm very proud of you, honey."

She smiled at him, a little embarrassed. "Laura would have done the same thing for me."

"And another thing," he continued, "that young man, David—he has the makings of a real horseman."

Mandy looked up quickly at the mention of David's name.

"Why, he's personally taken care of Solana ever since you've been catching up on your rest. He's groomed her, fed her, exercised her—taken real good care of her. And I don't think she'll have any problems with Founder again if you're careful."

"Oh, Daddy, I'm so glad. I never wanted Solana to suffer."

Mandy was happy that it had all turned out well. But she was anxious to see and talk to Laura as soon as possible. She hung around the Callahans' the next day, waiting for them to bring Laura home from the hospital.

Seeing them carry Laura into the house made Mandy's heart lurch. The cast looked so big and heavy. It covered Laura's entire leg from the thigh to her ankle. After Mandy was sure Laura was tucked comfortably into bed, she rapped gently on Laura's bedroom door.

"Come in," Laura called.

"Hi," Mandy said a little shyly.

"Hi," Laura returned. "Come sit down by my bed."

Funny, Mandy thought. They'd been friends for so long. They had lived through a nightmare together. Now they were acting like strangers.

"Thanks, Mandy," Laura said. She sensed the awkwardness between them, too. "I'm so glad you found me out there and stayed with me. I don't remember much, but I do remember that you were there."

"What are friends for?" Mandy shrugged, embarrassed.

"Well, I guess that finished it for me and the

fall riding show circuit." Laura changed the subject sadly.

"No way!" Mandy said emphatically.

"What do you mean? I can't train Diablo like this."

"No, but I can," Mandy said. "Look, Dad says Diablo's leg will be fine in a few days. We've worked together with him for years. I know I can work with him and keep him prime for the season." Mandy's eyes were shining.

"B-but what about Solana?"

"So, she can tag along. Maybe she'll learn a few things. Maybe she'll start acting more like a horse and less like a puppy." Mandy laughed.

"You'll need help . . . ," Laura protested.

Mandy took a deep breath, "David will help. He already said he would. At least until school starts and he gets interested in other things."

"Do you think you could?" Laura began to sound excited.

"You bet I can!" Mandy said.

"I think that would be great. I really want to continue my show riding," Laura admitted.

"And I'd like to see that wall covered with ribbons and trophies," Mandy added, pointing to Laura's trophy shelf.

"You really are my best friend," Laura told her.

"And you're mine," Mandy said. "Now, I'm going to go out there and take that horse of yours out for some exercise. After all, I think he and I had better get reacquainted."

Mandy left the bedroom, headed down the hall and out into the bright afternoon sunlight. On the far side of the lawn, she saw Solana grazing contentedly. Diablo stood tethered outside his stall. David was washing him down with a hose and brush. He looked over at Mandy. He smiled and waved.

Mandy took a deep breath. Then she headed toward the stables, her spirits soaring and her heart singing.

About Paso Finos

Paso Finos have been called the smoothest riding horses in the world. Columbus selected twenty stallions and five brood mares to come with him on his second voyage to the New World. The horses were a mixture of Spanish Barbs, Andalusians, and Jennets. In the New World, these horses became the foundation stock for breeding the future mounts of the conquistadors. These horses traveled great distances. They carried men in heavy armor over rough terrain. But the animals were agile, surefooted, and strong. Their smooth and comfortable gait made them highly prized by their owners.

Today's Paso Fino is also a much-prized and popular animal. The Paso is both distinctive and graceful. The Paso measures from 13 to 15 hands and weighs from 700 to 1100 pounds. Shoulders are sloping and deep, the rump well-rounded. Legs are straight and rather delicate in appearance. The hooves are small and sure. Pasos come in all colors, with and without white markings. But it is their unusual and smooth flowing gait that sets them apart from all other saddle horses.

For more information, contact: Paso Fino Horse Association, Inc., 101 North Collins Street, Plant City, Florida 33563-3311.

About the Author

LURLENE McDANIEL made up her first story in second grade, wrote a play in fourth grade, and wrote a book in high school.

Young readers from all over the country write to Lurlene to say how much they enjoy her books. They often ask the question, "Where do you get your ideas?" Lurlene says that ideas are everywhere. She uses her family and friends as character samples. She also gets ideas from television and newspapers and from her own interests, such as a fondness for horses.

Books about kids overcoming sensitive problems like cancer, diabetes, and divorce draw a wide response from her readers. Yet, Lurlene says the highest compliment a reader can give her is, "Your story was so interesting I couldn't put it down." Lurlene adds that basically that's what writing is all about—creating an uplifting story that causes the reader to look at life from a different perspective.

Other books by Lurlene McDaniel include *Six Months to Live, If I Should Die Before I Wake,* and *My Secret Boyfriend.*